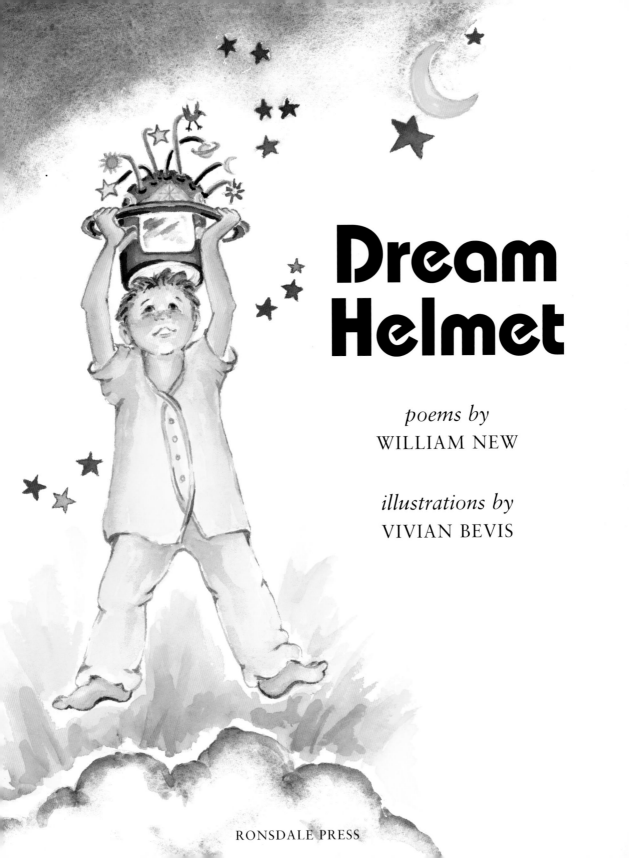

Dream Helmet

poems by
WILLIAM NEW

illustrations by
VIVIAN BEVIS

RONSDALE PRESS

Dream Helmet

If you lie down to sleep
with a dream helmet on
you can slip out to sea
on a night galleon —

With a dream helmet on
you are king of the sea,
the snow-covered mountains,
the air — or all three —

If you're king of the sea
you can swim to Peru —
no-one can say
what you can or can't do —

You can bike to Bermuda —
be king of the snow —
race on your skateboard
to planets below —

You can snowboard to Pluto
or dance the fandango
or juggle six oranges
high with a mango —

Dancing or juggling,
skating or not,
with a dream helmet on
you will never be caught —

For you're king
of the mountain-bike hills
and the air — and king of the sea —
you can dream your way there —

You can ski every hill,
you can hold every curve,
you can dance, you can dodge,
you can swim, you can swerve —

And around every curve
is a rippling stream
to an ocean of stars
where you lie down to dream

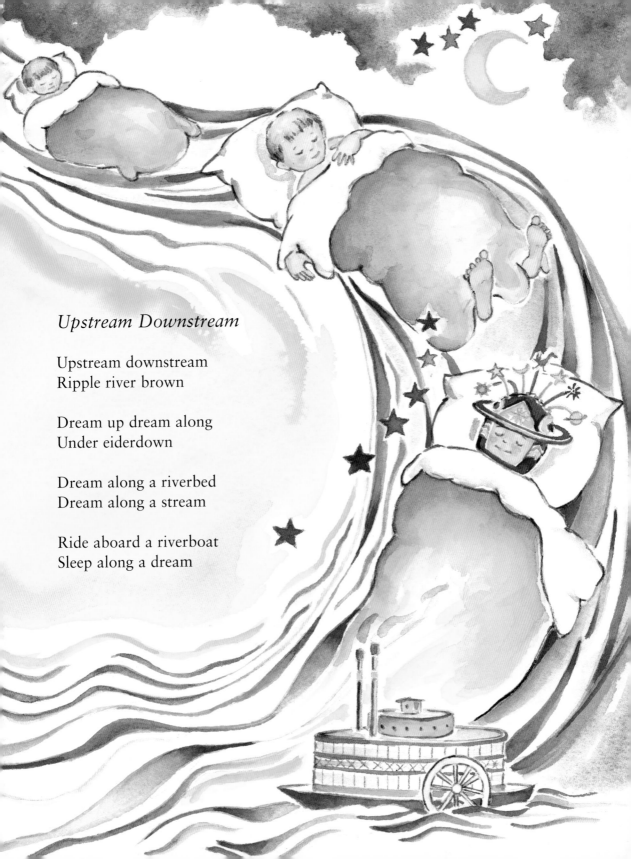

Upstream Downstream

Upstream downstream
Ripple river brown

Dream up dream along
Under eiderdown

Dream along a riverbed
Dream along a stream

Ride aboard a riverboat
Sleep along a dream

Super Seal

Who can scoot
down a shoot-the-chute?
a super seal
in a birthday suit —

a seal who dips
and yawns and flips,
who romps and rolls
the waves, who zips

up from the deeps,
who skips and leaps,
who somersaults
and never sleeps —

I can see you
waving back —
I think you'd like
to piggyback —

so can you swim
with a super seal?
in overdrive
you'll leap and wheel

and dive
        and shoot-the-chute and chase
so fast you'll scoot
to outer space —

How My Baby Brother Eats

I keep dreaming of volcanoes
pitching magma at the sky,
potatoes and tomatoes
and bananaskins that fly

And I know why: it's all because
my baby brother eats
his supper with a sloppy spoon
and both his hands and feet

He drips and drools and dribbles, smears
his food into his hair —
it's matted on his chin and crusted
underneath his chair

You wipe him up, you wipe him down,
his supper plate unloads —
I think he doesn't really eat,
the supper just explodes

How Big Are You?

1, 2,
How big are you?
As small as a button
As big as a clue —

3 and a quarter
3 and a half
Tall as a damson-dappled
giraffe —

4 grows high and
5 grows higher
Turtle and terrapin
Tapir and tiger —

6 is the size of an eagle, soaring —
7's the size of a lion, roaring —
  Always fast and fierce and strong,
  Always bursting into song —

    8's enormous
    9's gigantic
      10 is as tall as the mountain
      Megantic —

        stretching up
        and stretching high
          over the roof
          and into the sky,

            and just off the edge of this page
            with a kite
              are 11 and 12,
              who have grown out of sight —

A Round About Above Below

I want to sing a round about
a circulating roundabout —

and about a colt with a golden bell,
who rides a painted carousel —

the colt careens, and gallops free
of circle and calliope —

then leaps into the air and races —
with the stars it changes places —

open sky above — below
all dragonfly and indigo —

you hear? the echo of the bell
still sounds around the carousel

and all the colts who listen here
can leap into the atmosphere —

around the stars they rendezvous —
as far as Mars they chase the blue —

so tag along, and leap as high
as you can reach above the sky,

and join the gentle horses, springing
round about the starlight, singing —

Elephant Seal

At the midsummer dance in the firemen's hall
the walrus danced with everyone tall
except with the elephant seal —

The walrus danced with a red giraffe,
a jumping jay and a jersey calf
and even a hydro-electric eel
but not with the elephant seal —

The walrus danced the polka, the waltz —
he tapped and twirled — and true or false,
I've heard it said there was such a din
he even danced with a tuna tin —
but not with the elephant seal —

Do you think the elephant seal was sad?
Not on your life. Nor was she mad.
The elephant seal said *Thank you, no* —
I've seen you dance on everyone's toes
except on your own — *I'm happier here*
out on the ice with a ginger beer —
you can kick up your heels with a frog if you wish,
a moose or a mouse or a goggle-eyed fish,
a dog or even a doggerel dish,
but not with the elephant seal —

Fussing over nothing

A happy hippopotamus,
as garrulous and marvelous
as monkeys wearing cardigans
and buckled shoes regardless of
the weather, played the lead guitar
in an aqua-band in Boston Bar:

He talked a lot of calculus,
tyrannosauruses, the fuss
that octopuses make, and food.

I'm dubious that that was shrewd.

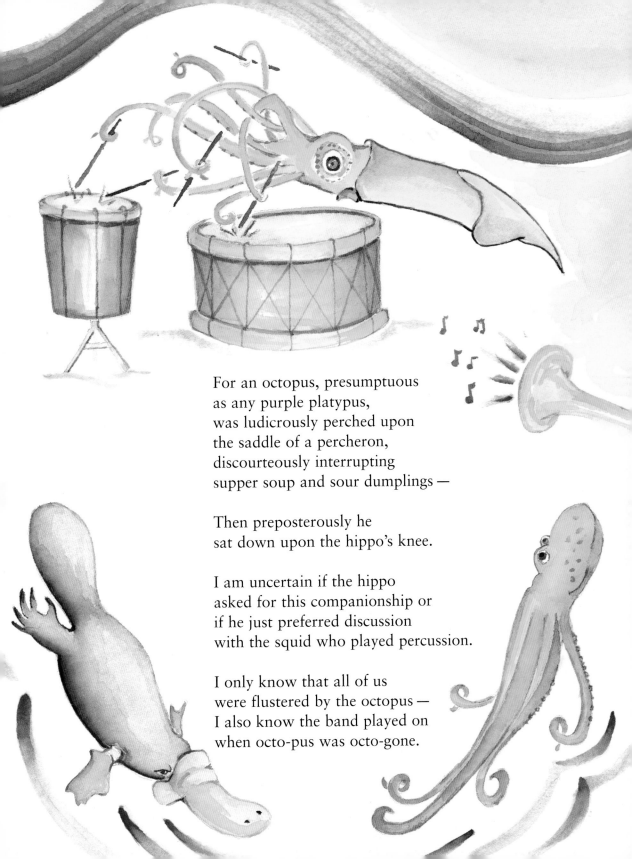

For an octopus, presumptuous
as any purple platypus,
was ludicrously perched upon
the saddle of a percheron,
discourteously interrupting
supper soup and sour dumplings —

Then preposterously he
sat down upon the hippo's knee.

I am uncertain if the hippo
asked for this companionship or
if he just preferred discussion
with the squid who played percussion.

I only know that all of us
were flustered by the octopus —
I also know the band played on
when octo-pus was octo-gone.

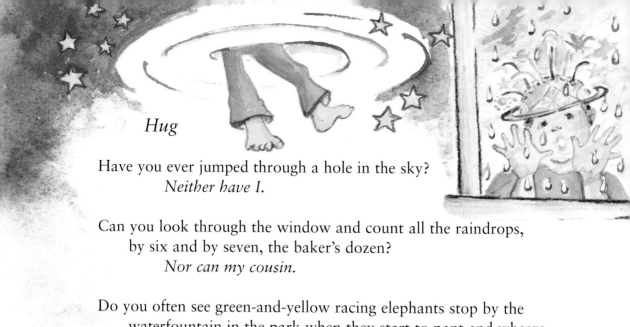

Hug

Have you ever jumped through a hole in the sky?
　　Neither have I.

Can you look through the window and count all the raindrops,
　　by six and by seven, the baker's dozen?
　　　　Nor can my cousin.

Do you often see green-and-yellow racing elephants stop by the
　　waterfountain in the park when they start to pant and wheeze,
　　for lemonade and a bit of a breather?
　　　　I don't either.

　　　　　　Has someone special hugged you today?
　　　　　　Now they have —
　　　　　　　　HURRAY!!!

The Knock-Kneed Knight

What should a knock-kneed knight have done
when his tights were tight and he couldn't run?

Maybe he ought to have bought some more
with the dough he earned at the pastry store —

or thought of something else — perhaps
sought to borrow before he collapsed,

or brought a second pair, or laughed
while he wrought a set by handicraft —

But the knight did not use sleight-of-hand,
or knit, or knot, or take command,

or trot to the slough-side Mall to swap
the too-tight pair at the Right Tight Shop —

Distraught, he shouted *I want out* —
Fraught, he dithered in a drought

of commonsense solutions — *Ow,*
he bellowed at a bough

he stumbled into — Rough and tough,
this mighty knight said *That's Enough,*

I'm weighing anchor — Night is near,
I'll nab the next sleigh out of here!

So he did naught to end his plight,
this knight in flight from his too-tight tights —

Indeed, throughout this frightful tale
a bit more light might have helped as well —

Instead of finding drought, he should have
used his brain to reign — he could have —

For really the knight was quite a charmer —
although his tights were made of armour —

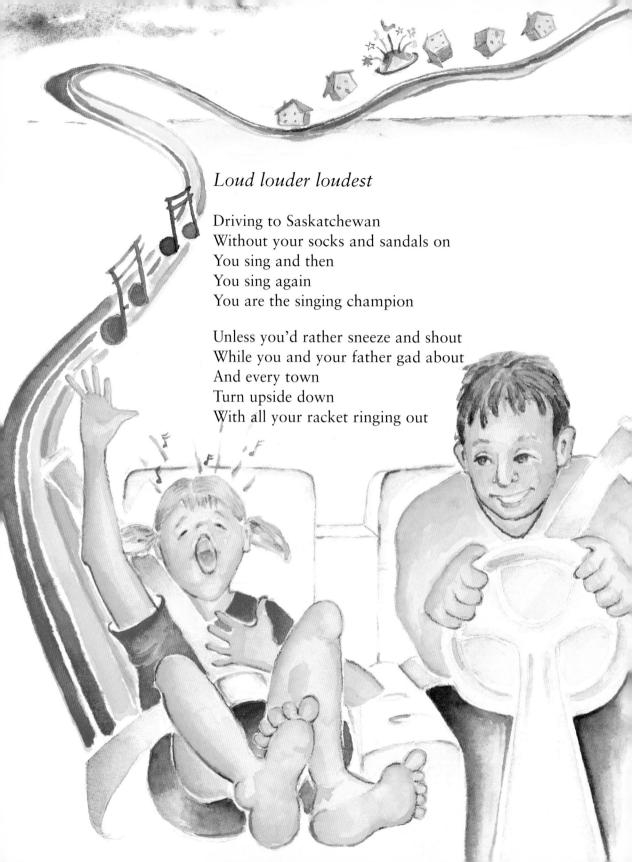

Loud louder loudest

Driving to Saskatchewan
Without your socks and sandals on
You sing and then
You sing again
You are the singing champion

Unless you'd rather sneeze and shout
While you and your father gad about
And every town
Turn upside down
With all your racket ringing out

"Is that as loud as you can sing?"
Your father asks — "A blistering
Magnifico
Fortissimo
Is loud — I think you're whispering —

"Even the socks that you abandoned
with your fossilizing sandals
In Alberta
Could exert a
Louder clamour single-handed —"

So then **SASKATCHEWAN** you sneeze —
So loud they hear you overseas:
On Jupiter
They're loopier
Because of you — and all the trees

Are losing leaves — Your father then
Says "*That* was utterly immense —
I'm sure I've heard
The loudest word
In history. Say it again!"

**SA
SKA
TCHEW
AN!!**

Tuque Talk

Tic tac tuque
Wintertime in Sooke

Tech talk turtleneck
En hiver au vieux Québec

Tick tock tackle tactic
Wintertime in Tuktoyaktuk

Great Lake Rag

Hereupon thereupon
Huron and Erie
Feeling quite put upon
Cold and contrary
Ontario shimmers
Superior storms
Kiss again Michigan
Winter turns warm

THUMBNAIL Sketch

Dear Grandma, thank you for the birthday gift.
I got it home **BONE** dry, lifting it
carefully in and out of the **TRUNK**, and nothing much
happened along the way except just before lunch,
along the **ARM** of the inlet, close to the
MOUTH of the river
near where the rose **HIPS** grow, we came over
the **BROW** of the hill where the factory outlet
BACKS onto the highway —
you know, where they sell the big sacks
of **KIDNEY** beans and **GUM**boots and **FINGER**paints? —
anyway, a big fir
LIMB fell into the road and missed us by a **WHISKER** —
we had to swerve out onto the **SHOULDER**
and just by the **SKIN** of our **TEETH** managed to
LUNGe over
onto the **CROWN** again — boy, was there ever
a bottle**NECK** then, w**HEELS** squealing and horns
blasting
and cars skidding
and s**LIP**ping
and shrieking
and stopping —

and everyone MUSCLEd out of their cars,
rANKLEd and out of JOINT, and tried to catch
the EARS of everyone else, and stood around EYEBALL
to EYEBALL, splitting HAIRS and blaming each other,
too CHEEKy altogether, TONGUES LASHing and wagging
until the lady from the GUMboot store managed to put a
LID on it — she RIBbed all the drivers, gave them pepper-
mints and cheaP ALMonds, and shoehorned them one by
one into separate lanes — and sort of half-HEARTedly,
with their unstARCHed shirt-tails hanging out, they all
began to KNUCKLE down
and TOE the line —

"Push your stARTER You're on your way," she yelled,
and other things in that VEIN, "SO LEt's hear those
engines" — and preSTO, MACHines began to roar
and go faster tHAN Dirt down a drain — you should
have seen the cars hightailing out of there, as they
NOSEd in and out of traffic, trailing 8-FOOT-high
motor homes, there were deLIVERy vans, threSHINg
maCHINes, towtrucks, and — well, finally after that
we HEADed home to ELBOW — I read billboards
all the way, and on the last LEG, as I said,
nothing much happened.

Your present's on the shelf
beside the toy **CHEST**. I put it there myself.
It didn't **WRINKLE**. And it's just what the train trac**K NEE**ded.
Every**BODY** sends their love —
xxx

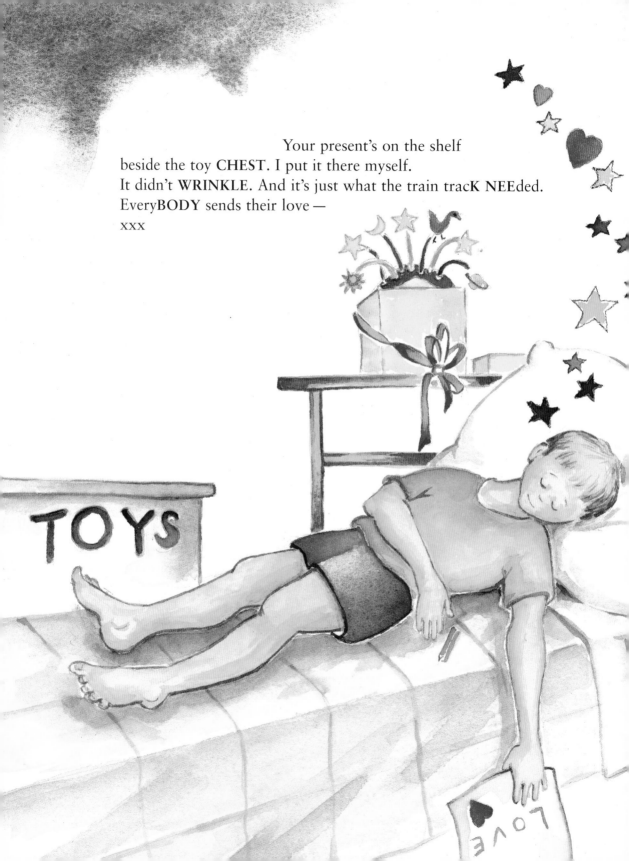

Elephant Walk

Ambling elephant
where do you walk —

from Kleena Kleene
to Plaster Rock —

under the overpass,
over the hill,
between the trees
in Vegreville —

up to the monkeybars,
close to the slide,
beneath the jungle
gym, beside

the waterfountain
in the park,
where I squirt my uncle
just for a lark —

Ambling elephant
take me along,
bellowing beautiful
elephant songs,

across the equator
and over the pole
(lingering longer
in Ingersoll)

to Come-by-Chance
and Harbour Grace,
Tatamagouche
and Parker Place —

through thick and thin
and Portage-la-Prairie
we'll amble as far
as necessary —

we won't be bothered
by sun and rain
or dirty feet
or hurricane —

staying away
from automobiles,
we'll lope and lumber,
saunter and wheel —

we'll amble afar
as off we roam,
then slowly slowly
amble home

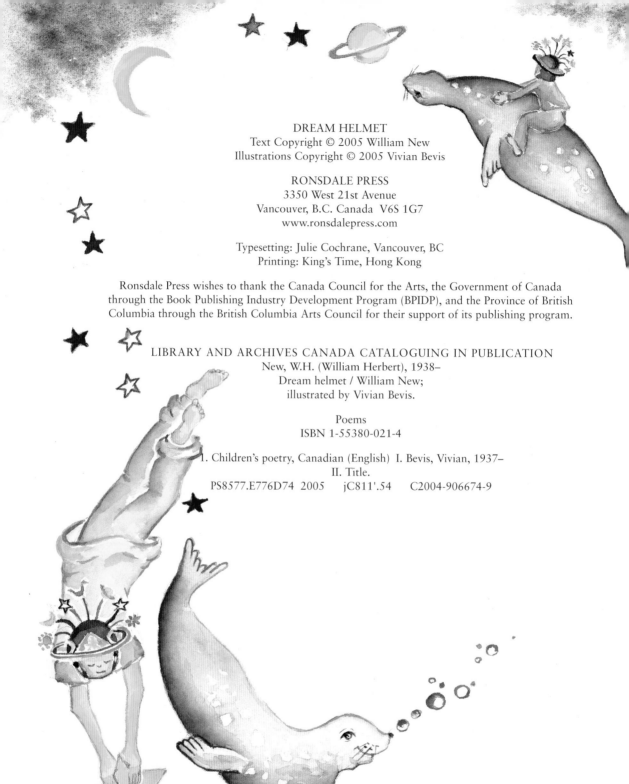

RONSDALE PRESS
3350 West 21st Avenue
Vancouver, B.C. Canada V6S 1G7
www.ronsdalepress.com

Typesetting: Julie Cochrane, Vancouver, BC
Printing: King's Time, Hong Kong

Ronsdale Press wishes to thank the Canada Council for the Arts, the Government of Canada
through the Book Publishing Industry Development Program (BPIDP), and the Province of British
Columbia through the British Columbia Arts Council for their support of its publishing program.

LIBRARY AND ARCHIVES CANADA CATALOGUING IN PUBLICATION
New, W.H. (William Herbert), 1938–
Dream helmet / William New;
illustrated by Vivian Bevis.

Poems
ISBN 1-55380-021-4

1. Children's poetry, Canadian (English) I. Bevis, Vivian, 1937–
II. Title.
PS8577.E776D74 2005   jC811'.54   C2004-906674-9